This book belongs to

....

For Hannah, Jessica, Ava and Yasmin.
You're awesome! – D.D.

For my son, for opening up a new world for me. – N.P.

First published 2022 by Macmillan Children's Books
an imprint of Pan Macmillan
The Smithson, 6 Briset Street, London, EC1M 5NR
EU representative: Macmillan Publishers Ireland Limited
1st Floor, The Liffey Trust Centre, 117–126 Sheriff Street Upper,
Dublin 1, D01 YC43
Associated companies throughout the world
www.panmacmillan.com

ISBN: 978-1-5290-6976-1

Text copyright © Donna David 2022
Illustrations copyright © Nina Pirhonen 2022
Nina Pirhonen would like to thank Grafia (Association of Visual
Communication Designers in Finland) for supporting this book.

1 3 5 7 9 8 6 4 2

A CIP catalogue record for this book is available from the British Library.

Printed in China

Donna David   Nina Pirhonen

CARS CARS CARS!

Find your favourite!

Macmillan Children's Books

Fast cars

Slow cars

Ready, steady, GO cars

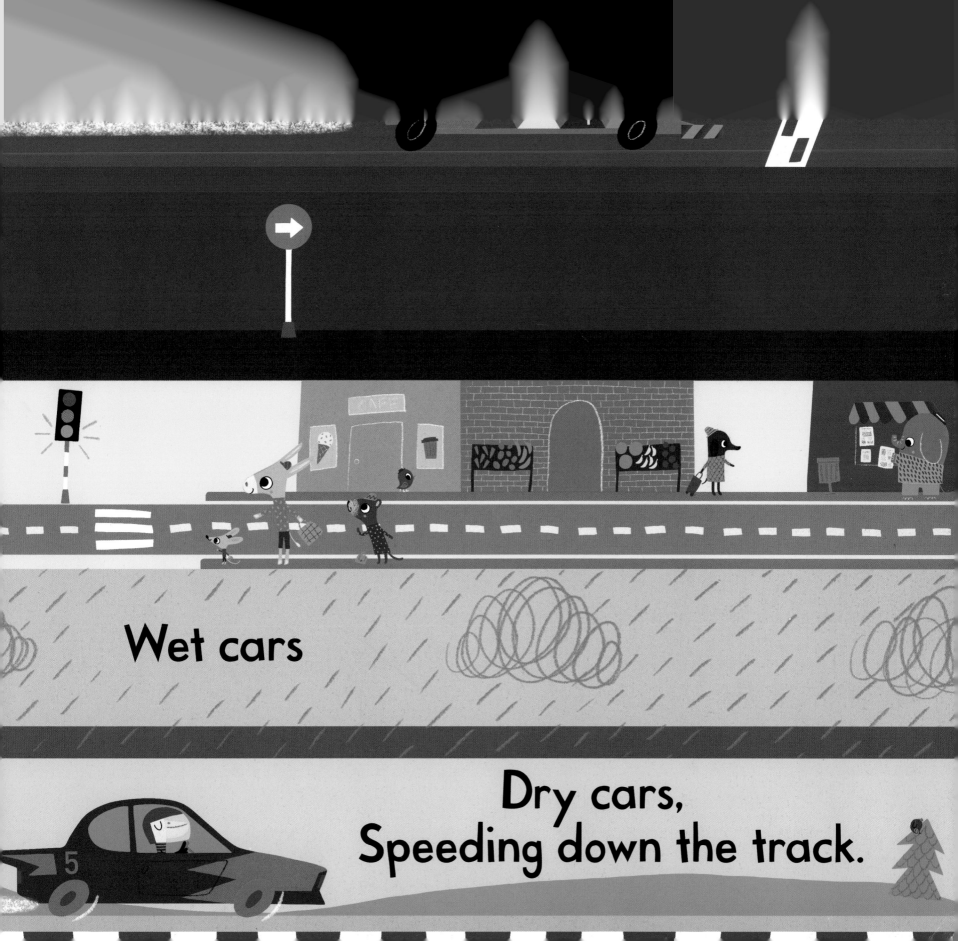

Wet cars

Dry cars,
Speeding down the track.

Old cars

New cars

Waiting in a queue cars

Swerving left and right cars

This one needs a jack!

STOP

Big cars

11

Small cars

30

Climbing up the wall cars

13

Quiet cars

Loud cars,
Bopping to the beat.

Long cars

Short cars

Snazzy-looking sports cars

Lined up at the park cars,

Powered by your feet!

Dirty cars

Clean cars

Hard to be
seen cars

Here to pick you up cars,
And take you home at night.

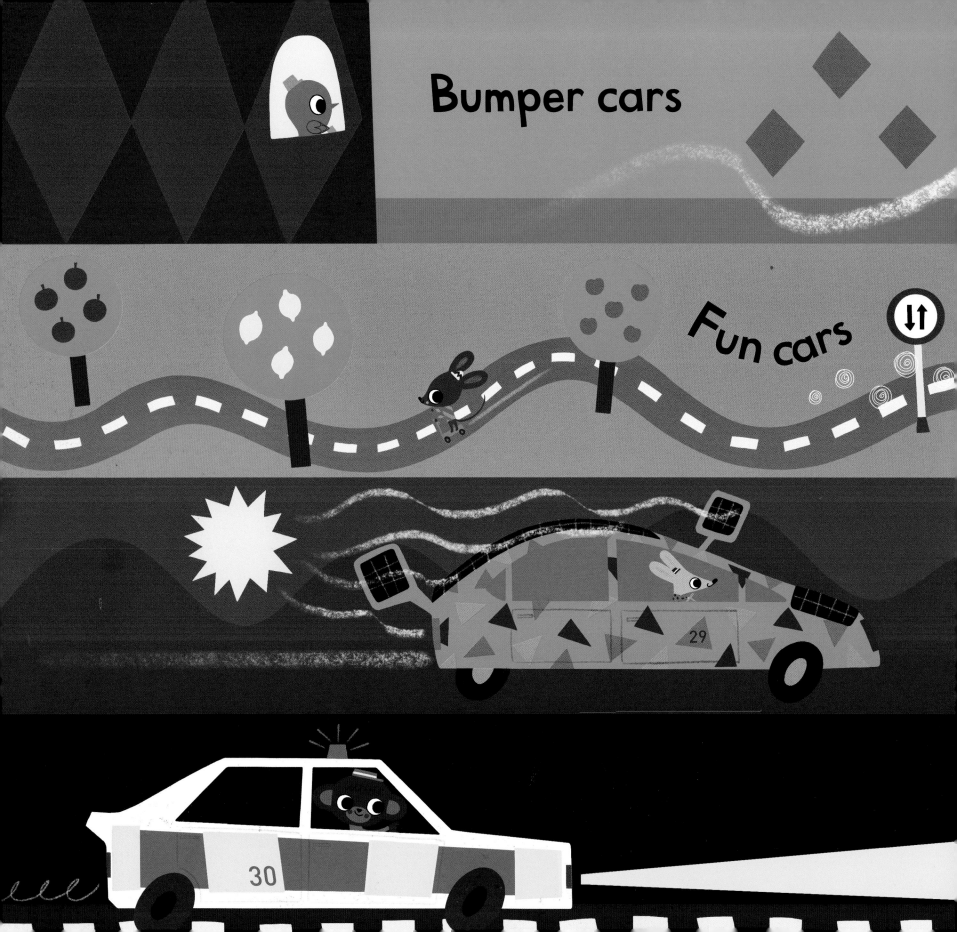

Bumper cars

Fun cars

Powered by the sun cars

Ready to give chase cars,
With a flashing light.

Up cars

Down cars

31

32

Driving into town cars

Collect all your kit cars,
Build them with a friend.

Right cars

Wrong cars

Pulling you along cars

Driving in the ice cars,
Skidding round the bend!

Tiny cars

Mighty cars

All strapped in
so tightly cars

Open top and windy cars,
Racing with the rest.

Here cars, there cars,
Going everywhere cars!
Try and count them all cars . . .

Which do you like best?

Did You Spot..?

Look back through the book
and see if you can find all these things!

 **A dog going shopping**
(near car number 3)

 **A skateboarding pelican**
(near car number 11)

 **A yummy cake**
(in car number 16)

 **A pair of owls**
(near car number 21)

 **A bubbly bucket**
(near car number 22)

 **A bird on a bike**
(near car number 28)

 **A mouse in a boat**
(near car number 31)

 **A toolbox**
(near car number 35)

 **A snowboarding spider**
(near car number 38)

 **A leopard in a ski lift**
(near car number 40)

  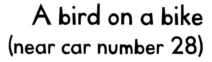

What else can you spot?

Reading Together
Tips for Parents and Carers

This book has been specifically created for preschool children. There is plenty of evidence to show that sharing books and reading together helps children to communicate, develop ideas and understanding, and gives them a head start at school. But the most important thing is to enjoy the closeness of sharing a book together.

- You can read *Cars Cars Cars* from start to finish, but you can also **dip in and out** just to look at the pictures.

- The fun, repetitive and rhythmic text **aids language learning and vocabulary.**

- Each car is numbered, to help number recognition and **counting skills.**

- The cars running across the page help your child get used to 'reading' from left to right and **turning the pages of a book.**

- The words and pictures are playful and fun. **Learning through play can be incredibly effective** – your child will be most receptive to new ideas and concepts if they are enjoying themselves.

- Perfect for sharing – reading together is a great way of spending time with your child. It can start new conversations, aid learning, and **develops listening, concentration and vocabulary skills.**

When you read this book together, you could talk to your child about . . .

. . . the numbers on the cars — which ones can they recognise? If they are more confident with numbers, **count along with your child from 1 to 10**, or even up to 50!

. . . the **words used to describe each car**. Which do they like best? Can your child come up with any more funny or unusual kinds of car?

. . . their own experiences and opinions. Use the cars in the book as **a starting point for new conversations**. Where would they like to go? How would they get there? What would they see along the way?

. . . other things they can spot. Try the **'Did you spot'** activity on the previous page. Then try making up your own, choosing different things for your child to find. Can they choose some things for you to spot, too?